d by American Girl Publishing, Inc.
ht © 2010 by American Girl, LLC

s reserved. No part of this book may be used or reproduced in any
whatsoever without written permission except in the case of brief
ns embodied in critical articles and reviews.

ns or comments? Call 1-800-845-0005, visit our Web site at
ngirl.com, or write to Customer Service, American Girl,
rway Place, Middleton, WI 53562-0497.

in China
2 13 14 15 LEO 10 9 8 7 6 5 4 3 2 1

rican Girl and Innerstar University marks, Amber™, Emmy™,
, Logan™, Neely™, Paige™, Riley™, and Shelby™ are trademarks
ican Girl, LLC.

ok is a work of fiction. Any similarity to real persons, living or dead,
dental and not intended by American Girl. References to real events,
or places are used fictitiously. Other names, characters, places, and
s are the products of imagination.

ed by Thu Thai at Arcana Studios

thanks to Katherine Van Sicklen-Holmes, USDF L Graduate Judge, USDF
te Instructor, BHSI Instructor, and USDF Silver Medalist

ing-in-Publication Data available from the Library of Congress.

Taking the Reins

by Alison Hart

illustrated by Arcana Studi

★ American Girl®

Publ
Copy

All r
man
quot

Ques
amer
8400

Print
10 11

All A
Isabe
of An

This
is co
peop
incid

Illus

Speci
Assoc

Catal

FAIRMONT
4330
Pasaden

INNERSTARU.COM

Welcome to Innerstar University! At this imaginary, one-of-a-kind school, you can live with your friends in a dorm called Brightstar House and find lots of fun ways to let your true talents shine. Your friends at Innerstar U will help you find your way through some challenging situations, too.

When you reach a page in this book that asks you to make a decision, choose carefully. The decisions you make will lead to more than 20 different endings! (*Hint:* Use a pencil to check off your choices. That way, you'll never read the same story twice.)

Want to try another ending? Read the book again—and then again. Find out what would have happened if you'd made *different* choices. Then head to www.innerstarU.com for even more book endings, games, and fun with friends.

Innerstar Guides

Every girl needs a few good friends to help her find her way. These are the friends who are always there for **you**.

Emmy

A brave girl who loves swimming and boating

Isabel

A confident girl with a funky sense of style

Riley

A good sport, on the field and off

Paige

A nature lover who leads hikes and campus cleanups

Amber

An animal lover and
a loyal friend

Neely

A creative girl who loves
dance, music, and art

Logan

A super-smart girl
who is curious about
EVERYTHING

Shelby

A kind girl who is there
for her friends—and loves
making NEW friends!

Innerstar U Campus

1. Rising Star Stables
2. Star Student Center
3. Brightstar House

4. Starlight Library
5. Sparkle Studios
6. Blue Sky Nature Center

7. Real Spirit Center
8. Five-Points Plaza
9. Starfire Lake & Boathouse
10. U-Shine Hall

11. Good Sports Center
12. Shopping Square
13. The Market
14. Morningstar Meadow

★ 9 ★

F ollow me!" Riley calls.
You tug on the right rein, steering your horse
into the woods behind the other riders. Riley and
her paint horse Rio lead the way, just behind one of the
Innerstar U riding instructors. Devin rides her young
Thoroughbred, Fleet, and Shelby follows on quiet Comet.
You're riding your favorite horse, Angel.

"This way!" you call to Amber, who is riding behind
you on a spunky horse named Silver Sky.

You grin as you trot Angel through the woods that
surround the beautiful Innerstar U campus. The wind
brushes your cheeks. The sun, peeking through the leaves,
dapples the trail. Angel's ears prick as she trots. She's
enjoying the ride as much as you are.

 Turn to page 11.

"There's a jump ahead!" the instructor warns. A log is lying across the trail. One by one, the horses in front of you take the jump. Just before you reach the log, you lean forward. You squeeze your heels into Angel's sides, and she takes off, soaring over the log. You laugh with delight when Angel lands and trots after Comet.

"Whoa! Whoa!" you suddenly hear Amber holler from behind you.

You halt Angel and look over your shoulder. Amber is sprawled on the ground. "Amber's hurt!" you call to the others.

Quickly, you dismount and lead Angel back to Amber. Silver Sky snorts as you approach. You know the gray horse can be a handful. Did he buck Amber off?

"What happened?" you ask Amber. "Are you okay?"

"Sky stumbled after the jump, and I fell off," Amber tells you. Her face is pale, and she's holding her wrist.

After a quick look, the instructor decides to walk Amber to the student health center, which is about a quarter mile down the trail. She leads both horses by the reins and asks the rest of you to return—carefully—to Rising Star Stables. You wave sadly at Amber as she heads down the trail, cradling her wrist in her other arm.

"I hope she'll be all right," you say softly.

"Me, too!" Devin exclaims. "Next week is the horse show. If Amber can't ride, the Innerstar U team will lose."

Turn to page 12.

"Silver Sky is the best horse on the team," Devin says. "Besides Fleet." She pats her beautiful chestnut horse. "The team needs Amber and Sky to win points."

"Is that the only reason you hope Amber is okay?" Riley asks. She and Shelby are on the Innerstar U team, too.

"Of course not," Devin replies with a toss of her head. "I'm just saying the team needs her to win."

You roll your eyes, glad you decided not to compete in the show. You love riding, and you're one of the better riders at school. But the last show you rode in was a disaster. You were riding a spunky horse like Silver Sky. When he refused a jump, you fell off, landing in a heap at the judge's feet.

That day, you lost your confidence in jumping and showing. Then the riding instructor paired you up with gentle, steady Angel. Now you love jumping again—but only on the trail.

As you head back toward Rising Star Stables, Devin is still talking about the upcoming show. "Innerstar U *has* to beat Hillside School's riding team," she says hotly. "We can't lose to them two years in a row."

Just hearing about the show makes you feel sick. *No showing for me,* you vow. You would only let the team down.

The next day you head to the stables to ride again. You're thrilled to find Amber there, along with some of the other riders. It turns out that Amber's wrist was fractured, so she's wearing a cast on it.

"The doctor said I won't be able to ride for three months," Amber says with a grimace.

"Three months!" Riley exclaims.

Devin groans. "But the team needs four horses and riders," she says. "We can't win without you and Sky."

"Sky can still be in the show," Amber says. "He just needs a new rider."

"Who?" Shelby asks.

You're wondering the same thing. You turn to face Amber. Her brown eyes seem to smile as she says, "You!"

Your jaw drops. "Me?" you squeak.

"You're one of the best riders at school," Amber says, "and one of the best jumpers."

Shelby gives you an encouraging smile. "Yesterday you and Angel popped that log perfectly," she says.

"B-but," you stammer, "that was on the trail."

"You'd be a great rider for Silver Sky," Riley says. "And the team needs you. Will you do it?"

All the girls stare at you, waiting for your answer. You're terrified, but you don't want to admit in front of everyone that you're too chicken to compete in the show.

If you blurt, "Of course I'll ride Sky," go to page 14.

If you thank Amber but tell her, "I'll have to think it over," turn to page 16.

You can't believe you said yes! Amber jumps up and gives you a hug. "I'm so glad," she says excitedly. "Silver Sky needs to be in the show, and you're a terrific rider."

"Umm, not terrific," you murmur as your stomach starts churning.

"With you on Silver Sky, Innerstar U can win!" Shelby adds. All four girls give you the school cheer.

You're not cheering. What if you let the team down?

Before you can say anything, Amber takes Angel's bridle from you and hangs it back up. "Come on," she says. "Let's groom Silver Sky. Then you can ride him. We need to start practicing right now. The show's only a week away!"

Turn to page 18.

"You can give me your answer tomorrow," Amber says. You nod, feeling numb. There's no way you want to ride in the competition. But the Innerstar U team needs four riders. How can you say no to your friends?

"I sure hope your answer will be yes!" Amber adds with a smile. Picking up a grooming box, she and Riley leave the tack room.

Devin gives you a sharp look. "I don't think you can handle Silver Sky," she says. "You're used to riding Angel. She's a sweetheart compared to Sky."

"Don't listen to Devin," Shelby tells you. "You're a great rider. You can handle Sky."

"Not with just a week of practice," Devin says, grabbing Fleet's bridle. "We want to win the competition, not lose."

"Well, without a fourth rider, we don't stand a chance," Shelby says hotly.

Your head snaps back and forth as you listen to Devin and Shelby. You're so confused that you don't know whom—or what—to believe.

 Turn to page 19.

FLEET ANGEL COMET R...

"Uh, don't you have to finish cleaning tack?" you ask. Everything is happening way too fast.

"We have all day for that," Amber says as she grabs a grooming box. As you follow her to the stalls, you tell yourself you can do this. The team needs a fourth rider, and Silver Sky is a terrific horse. You've ridden spirited horses before, right?

You stop in front of Sky's stall and peek inside. Amber is brushing him with her good arm. "Come on in," she calls.

When you step closer, Sky pins his ears. He's used to Amber, because she's been his main rider this year. But his ears are saying that he's not exactly happy to see *you*.

"Uh, hi, Sky," you say as you pick up a brush. Maybe grooming time will help him get to know you. But when it's time to bridle him up, Sky sticks his head high in the air, out of your reach. You sigh. Angel never acts this way. She's always so sweet. Maybe Sky just doesn't like you.

Amber doesn't seem to notice. She's still chattering away about what a great pair you and Sky will make. She helps you bridle and saddle him. He behaves for her.

But when you lead Sky from the stall, he almost runs over you. Sky is not gentle Angel, that's for sure. In fact, you think, he may be too much horse for you to handle.

 If you try to ride Sky anyway, turn to page 20.

 If you confess to Amber that you aren't the best rider for Sky, turn to page 21.

After Shelby and Devin leave the tack room, you're left alone with your thoughts. *Both girls are right,* you think. Sky is a handful, but you're a good rider.

Your churning stomach reminds you of that awful show when you fell off your horse. Do you have the nerve to ride in another competition?

That was months ago, you tell yourself. You should be getting over your fear by now, and what better way than to ride in Saturday's show? Besides, the team needs you!

After hanging up Angel's bridle, you hurry from the tack room into the barn. You find Amber in Sky's stall, putting a halter on him. The other girls are grooming their horses in the stalls nearby.

"Amber, I've made up my mind," you tell her. At that, Devin's head pops up over the wall. Shelby peeks into Sky's stall, too. All the girls stare at you expectantly. You hope that you sound confident, because deep inside, you're definitely not!

 Turn to page 24.

"It's okay, Sky," you whisper as you lead him out of the stable. "I know you don't like me as much as you like Amber. But let's try to be friends."

As you enter the arena, where Amber is waiting, your heart sinks. Four other riders, including Devin, are schooling—or training—their horses in the arena. They turn to watch you.

A show will be even worse. Dozens of people will be watching, just as they were watching the day you fell off at the judge's feet. *Ugh.*

"Come on!" Amber calls, waving you to the mounting block, where you can climb up into the saddle.

Sky paws with one hoof as if to say, *Yeah, let's get a move on!*

You suddenly feel frozen with fear.

 Turn to page 22.

"Amber, I don't know if it's a good idea for me to ride Sky," you tell her.

"Why?" she asks, sounding surprised.

You stare at your feet. "Last summer I rode a horse like Sky in a show, and he dumped me," you explain. "It was so embarrassing. My courage has been pretty shaky ever since."

Amber shrugs. "I've been dumped dozens of times," she says, holding up her cast. "So I understand totally. You shouldn't show Sky until you're ready."

You sigh with relief and nod.

"We'll start slow," says Amber. "How about if we work in one of the small, more private rings?"

"That sounds like a good idea," you say, and you hope it is. You're not sure Amber realizes how nervous you are.

But as you ride Sky around the ring, your nervousness disappears. He's responsive, with super-smooth gaits.

"Wow, Amber, I love Sky," you tell her at the end of the lesson. "Riding him is like a dream!"

 Turn to page 40.

You can do this, you tell yourself. You lead Sky to the mounting block. He switches his tail angrily when you tighten the girth around his belly.

Amber points to the far end of the arena. A small course of jumps is set up. "Sky is entered in two jumping classes in the show," she says.

Jumping! You should have known. In a jumping class, the horse has to clear all the fences to win. It can't knock down a rail, go off course, or refuse to jump.

You groan. You know all about refusing.

"How high are the fences in the classes?" you ask.

"Three feet," Amber replies. "Easy for Sky."

And easy for you before you fell off. You haven't jumped that high since that awful day.

Amber smiles. "Don't worry," she says. "We won't start that high. After you warm up Sky, we'll practice over a small crossbar."

That makes you feel a little better. You mount Sky awkwardly. When you touch his sides with your heels, he prances forward, eager to go. As you trot Sky in a circle, your heart starts pounding.

Amber walks over to a tiny crossbar. "Start by jumping over this," she suggests.

You think about all the things you should do to jump an obstacle successfully. Tip your upper body slightly forward. Look straight between Sky's ears. Put your weight in your heels. Hold the reins steady. You glance back at the crossbar as you circle Sky around the ring again.

"Hey! Watch where you're going!" someone yells.

You snap your head around. Sky is about to run into Fleet! Quickly, Devin steers Fleet to the left. You yank Sky to the right, avoiding a crash.

"Next time, pay attention," Devin says curtly.

"Sorry!" you call.

"Ready?" Amber calls to you. You take a deep breath, trying to calm down. But Sky tosses his head. He knows you're not Amber. And he knows you're not feeling very confident.

 If you decide that Silver Sky is too wound up to jump, turn to page 27.

 If you head to the crossbar anyway, turn to page 28.

You open your mouth, but the words "I'll ride Sky" get stuck. Instead you blurt, "I need to get to know Sky first. Devin's right. I'm used to riding Angel."

"That's a good idea," Amber says. "We can start today. Why don't you help me exercise Sky?"

As Amber leads Sky outside, he prances excitedly, showing off. He's beautiful—dappled gray and full of energy. You can see why the team wants Sky to compete in the show.

Since Amber's wrist is in the cast, she has trouble holding him steady. Taking a deep breath, you calm your fears. This is a good time to get to know spunky Sky and show him who's boss.

As you take the lead rope from Amber, Sky throws his head up and dances backward. The rope grows taut. He's testing you—trying to pull away.

You remind yourself that you've worked with spirited horses before. Holding the rope tightly, you walk toward Sky. "Easy, boy," you say.

When he halts, you pat his neck. But your heart is thumping. You managed to keep Sky under control, but are you confident enough to ride him?

If you try to ride Sky, turn to page 26.

If you stall for more time, turn to page 29.

As you help Amber tighten Sky's girth—the band placed around his belly to keep his saddle in place—you picture yourself mounted on him, holding a blue ribbon. You'd love to help the team win the upcoming competition.

Winning points for the team and making your friends happy—both are great reasons to ride in the show, right?

"Are you ready?" Amber asks. She's holding Silver Sky, waiting for you to mount him. Sky is staring at you with dark, flashing eyes. *Uh-oh.* You recognize that frisky gleam.

You think about Amber falling off yesterday on the trail. Maybe Sky *didn't* stumble.

The rosy picture of Sky sporting that blue ribbon pops like a balloon. *This isn't a dream,* you remind yourself. You can't wish yourself winning for the team. You have to do it. That means riding Sky, an unfamiliar horse. Then you have to ride in a show where everyone is watching you. Your confidence has been in the basement since that fall. You have to be realistic. Can you really do this?

If you buy yourself some time to try to boost your confidence, turn to page 31.

If you tell Amber that you can't ride in the show, turn to page 35.

You halt Sky in front of Amber. You need to tell her the truth. "I'm too nervous to jump Sky," you tell her. "And he knows it. I don't think he trusts me as a rider."

"Oh," says Amber. She seems surprised. Then Sky dances nervously in place. She strokes his neck, trying to calm him.

"I rode in a show last summer, and my horse refused a fence," you confess. "I fell off. I haven't jumped in a ring since then. And a nervous me on a nervous Sky could be a disaster."

Amber cocks her head as if she's thinking. "It *could* be a disaster," she finally says. "But it doesn't have to be. I have two ideas."

Amber tells you her ideas. You like both of them!

If you choose Amber's idea of entering Silver Sky in an easier class, turn to page 114.

If you choose Amber's idea of working hard to gain Silver Sky's trust, turn to page 30.

You circle Sky around the arena again. Your mouth is dry with fear. *Be confident,* you tell yourself. *It's only a little jump.*

You plaster a fake smile on your face. Amber gives you a thumbs-up. But Sky acts up, rushing his trot. Your smile might fool Amber, but it doesn't fool Sky. He knows you're scared of this teensy fence.

"You can do it!" Riley yells.

"Go, girl!" you hear Shelby call to you.

"Do it," Devin chimes in.

You snap your head around. Everyone is staring at you, just as if you were in a show.

Eek! Your pulse races as you aim Sky toward the cross-bar. It looks ten feet tall! What if he refuses in front of your friends and the other riders? That would almost be worse than during a real show.

 Turn to page 34.

You decide to lead Sky around the ring instead of riding him. That'll give you time to gather some courage. Then Sky stomps at a fly, stepping on your foot. Tears rush into your eyes.

You wiggle your toes. Nothing's broken, but a sore foot doesn't do anything to boost your courage.

Amber sucks in her breath. "Are you all right?" she asks.

"Sky stepped on my foot," you say, wincing. "But I'm okay." You don't tell her that you think Sky's a handful.

"Sorry," says Amber. "I'll spray him with fly spray." She hands you the lead line and hurries to the tack room.

Immediately Sky strides off after her. "Whoa, whoa," you say quickly. You sound like someone who has never worked with horses before. What's wrong with you? It's as if your lack of confidence is snowballing.

"Whoa." This time you say it as if you mean it. Sky halts and gives you a curious look. "Now stand here," you add.

When Amber comes out of the tack room with the spray, she says, "I need to know as soon as possible if you'll ride Sky. The show's Saturday. That's only a week to practice. Will you know by tomorrow?"

"Definitely," you tell her, but inside, you know there's nothing definite about your feelings. You love to ride, but you're not sure Sky is the right horse for you. Maybe talking to some of your other friends will help you decide.

 Turn to page 32.

"Building trust can be fun," Amber says. "Let's brainstorm some ideas."

You dismount and lead Sky back to the stall. As you and Amber untack him, you toss ideas back and forth. She suggests team games. You suggest a trail ride. Both would help you and Sky get to know each other.

You think more about the ideas as you lead Sky back outside and turn him out in a small pasture. The sun is bright and warm, making you feel better. Sky bucks and plays in the field. Again, you notice how gorgeous he is. You sure would love to show him Saturday.

You head back into the stable and help Amber clean Sky's stall.

"I love your idea of team games," you tell your friend. "Sky and I can bond. But the whole team can bond, too. That will be good for Saturday's show."

"And I like your idea of a trail ride. The whole team could go," Amber says. "Trail riding is what you love best. Sky loves it, too. It would be a good way to build trust."

Amber says the choice is yours, and it's a tough one. Both ideas sound fun to you.

 If you choose team games, turn to page 42.

 If you choose a team trail ride, go online to innerstarU.com/secret and enter this code: BCONFIDENT

"I left my helmet at the dorm," you tell Amber. It's true. Plus, going to get your helmet will give you some time to gather your courage.

While you run back to the dorm, you think about all the reasons why you should ride Sky in the show. You write them down when you get to your room. Then you tear out the list, fold it up, and slip it into your pocket, hoping it will give you the courage to get on that horse.

 Turn to page 36.

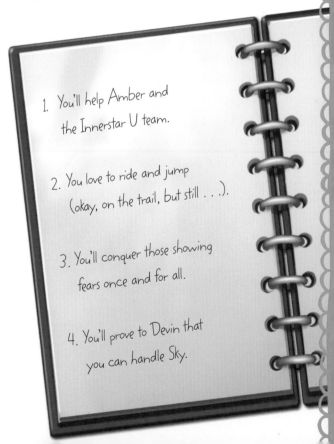

1. You'll help Amber and the Innerstar U team.

2. You love to ride and jump (okay, on the trail, but still . . .).

3. You'll conquer those showing fears once and for all.

4. You'll prove to Devin that you can handle Sky.

You hobble back to Brightstar House, where you find Shelby and Isabel hanging out in Isabel's room. Isabel is braiding Shelby's wavy hair into twisty braids.

"Hey, that looks cute," you say as you plop into Isabel's comfy chair.

"Thanks," Isabel says. "Want me to braid yours, too?"

You brush your hair off your forehead. "My hair is the least of my problems," you say with a sigh.

"What's wrong?" Shelby asks. Then she says, "I bet it has something to do with riding Sky in Saturday's show."

You nod glumly. "Amber really wants me to say yes," you explain. "Only the last time I was in a show, I fell off. It was a major disaster."

"I'm riding in the show, too," Shelby says. "And I bet I'm even more nervous than you. Hey!" She snaps her fingers. "I've got an idea that might help us both."

"I've got an even better idea," Isabel says, still eyeing your hair. "The perfect confidence booster—a funky new hairstyle."

 If you decide to ask equally nervous Shelby for her idea, turn to page 39.

 If you decide to let Isabel give you a new hairdo, turn to page 55.

You're so worried about looking stupid in front of your friends that you forget all about being a good rider. Your body goes rigid. You grip the reins tensely.

Sky tosses his head, and the reins slide through your sweaty fingers. You snatch them back up. "Enough of that, Sky," you snap. You won't let him refuse. You're going to show him who's boss, show him that you're not afraid.

Only Sky knows that you are. Throwing his head high, he bolts away from the crossbar.

 If you try to turn him in a tight circle so that he doesn't run off, turn to page 43.

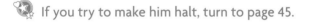 If you try to make him halt, turn to page 45.

"Amber, I'm sorry. I can't ride Sky in the show," you blurt.

"Why not?" she asks, her eyes wide.

"Because, um . . ." You think hard. "Well, my hunt coat is . . . old," you say. Okay, that's a terrible reason.

"You can borrow mine," Amber says. But then she cocks her head. She puts her hands on her hips and gives you a funny look. "What's the real reason?" she asks.

You let out your breath. You need to tell Amber the truth. "I don't think I can handle Sky," you admit. "He's a lot friskier than Angel."

"But you're a good rider," Amber says. "If you don't ride him, I'll have to scratch him from the show. And the team needs four riders and horses."

Your heart melts. If you don't say yes, you'll totally let Amber and the team down.

"I'm sorry," you say glumly, "but the truth is, I'm a little scared of Sky. And I'm really scared of jumping in a show ring. A week just isn't enough time to get over my fears."

Amber sighs. You feel terrible, knowing that you've disappointed her. But then she says, "Thanks for telling me. I totally understand. A week isn't very long."

The two of you untack Sky in silence. You picture the Hillside School riders winning the competition again this year. You imagine them waving the big trophy as they gloat. You wish you could still help out the Innerstar U team. But if you won't ride in the show, what can you do?

 Turn to page 37.

When you get back to the barn, you pat that slip of paper in your pocket. The list gives you the confidence to mount Sky and ride him around the ring.

Your first lesson goes well. Sky knows you're not Amber and tries to buck a couple of times, but you sit deep and make him behave. Afterward, you tell Amber, "If our next practice goes as well as that one, I'll ride Sky in the show."

Amber is delighted. "We'll practice all week," she says. "I just know you and Sky will be great together."

The next day, Amber gives you another lesson on Sky. Soon you're confidently trotting and cantering him.

Then Monday night, you have a nightmare. You're in the show ring cantering your horse toward a jump. The horse refuses. Only this time, the horse is Sky. You fly off, sailing through the air in slow motion. You fall at your teammates' feet, and they point at you and laugh.

You wake up in a sweat. What if that happens Saturday? You'll let Amber and your teammates down!

 Turn to page 38.

As the show grows nearer, you notice the girls on the team are rushing around trying to get ready. Tack needs scrubbing, boots need polishing, horses need bathing, and manes need braiding.

On Wednesday afternoon, you head to the stables to ride Angel. When you see Devin and Shelby in the tack room buried under bridles and reins, you ask, "Can I help?"

"Can you ever!" Devin exclaims as she hands you a bridle. Shelby tosses you a sponge, and you start scrubbing. When that's done, you hold Rio for Riley while she bathes him. She gets more soap on you than on her horse, which makes you both laugh.

Saturday morning, you're up bright and early with the others. You check braids, brush out tails, and give riders a boost into the saddle—and a boost of confidence before they go into the ring. That's when you realize that everyone on the team is nervous about showing, even Devin. It's not just you who gets scared.

Later, when the show's almost over, Devin says, "Thanks for your help."

Riley adds, "We couldn't have done it without you!"

And Shelby says, "Yup. You're one of the team now."

That makes you smile. Next show, you decide, you *will* be one of the team. Only instead of riding Sky, you'll tackle the show ring on Angel!

The End

The next day, Amber wants you to practice over a small jump course. You keep thinking about that nightmare. As you trot Sky toward the jump, you begin to tremble.

Sky tosses his head. He can feel your lack of confidence. He charges left, missing the jump.

"Hey, what happened?" Amber hollers. "Sky never runs out on a fence."

You can't tell Amber the truth—that you're not ready to face the fence.

"I lost a stirrup, so I turned Sky away from the jump," you fib. Your face grows hot with guilt. You hate not telling Amber the real reason—that you're so worried about Saturday's show, you're not a good partner for Sky.

"Try again," Amber says.

Nodding, you steer Sky toward the jump. You push the nightmare from your head—for Sky's and Amber's sake, you have to do this.

Sky clears the jump perfectly. "Great!" Amber says. "I'm going to raise it six inches."

Your stomach tightens. So far, you've managed to avoid those big jumps. Amber adjusts the rail and steps back. You trot Sky in a circle and then point him toward the jump. You gulp. Six inches seems like two feet higher!

 If you go for the jump anyway, turn to page 47.

 If you steer Sky away from the jump, turn to page 44.

"Let's be support buddies," Shelby suggests. "We can help each other get ready for the show, and we can cheer each other on. That would make me less nervous."

"Me, too," you say warmly. "I like your idea, Shelby!"

"Let's start tomorrow," Shelby says. "We'll ride in the ring together. You can give me pointers. I have so much trouble getting Comet into a smooth canter."

"And you can keep assuring me that I can jump Sky in the show," you tell your friend.

"That will be easy!" Shelby says with a big smile. "Because you can!"

You like Shelby's positive attitude. It's just what you needed to make up your mind. You meet Amber in the hall the next morning, and you tell her that you'll ride in the show.

"Yay! I'm so glad," Amber squeals, giving you a hug.

You nod excitedly. "Shelby and I are going to be support buddies," you say. "Is it okay if I ride Sky this afternoon?"

"Of course!" says Amber. "I can't wait." She links her arm with yours as you head down the steps.

 Turn to page 80.

"How's it going?" you hear someone yell. Riley, Shelby, and Devin come walking toward the ring.

Devin leans against the fence rail. "Ready to win a ribbon in Junior Jumper?" she asks. "We need those points."

Your heart skips a beat. Sky is a dream, but entering a show in one week feels more like a nightmare.

As the girls chatter about the show, the old dread creeps over you. Should you tell Amber you aren't ready? What if you enter the show and you don't win points? No matter what you do, you're bound to let your friends down.

If you tell Amber that you're not ready to compete, turn to page 46.

If you decide to fake confidence, turn to page 52.

The next day, after classes, the Innerstar U riding team meets at Five-Points Plaza to brainstorm team games. The five of you sit on the grass.

"I think we should have an Egg Race," Shelby suggests. "We used to do that in 4-H. The rider holds a boiled egg on a spoon while her horse walks, trots, and canters. Whoever can keep the egg on the spoon the longest wins!"

"Or how about Follow the Leader?" says Riley. "Each rider takes a turn being the leader. She can lead the group around the ring, on the trail—wherever she wants."

Then Amber explains Zigzag Cones: "You and your horse have to weave around cones set up in a zigzag," she says. "You're out if your horse knocks one down."

All these games sound great to you. How will the team choose just one?

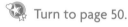 Turn to page 50.

Your heart drops into your stomach. Sky breaks into a gallop, heading straight for the other horses.

Fortunately, you know what to do when a horse runs off. You tug hard on the right rein, turning Sky. He misses the other horses and riders—just barely. You keep turning him in smaller circles until he slows to a trot. When Sky finally halts, you realize you're shaking all over.

Amber runs up. "Are you all right?"

"Fine," you gasp. "But I made a mistake. I'm not the right rider for Sky." Quickly you dismount and hand Amber the reins. Staring straight ahead, you stride from the ring. You're so embarrassed, your cheeks burn. Everyone is watching you leave. Everyone!

"Wait!" Amber calls as she tries to catch up with you. "I know Sky has a mind of his own. But you did stop him."

"Barely," you mutter. "What if that happens in a show?"

"With practice, you'll know how to handle him," Amber assures you.

Only now your confidence has sunk even lower. You should have told Amber the truth about being scared. You shouldn't have pretended to be ready. You rushed into jumping Sky, and you paid the price.

"Maybe next time," you mumble. You hope there will be a next time. But right now, you wish you could just disappear. You don't have the courage to face your friends, and you sure don't have the courage to get back on Sky again.

The End

Quickly, you steer Sky away from the jump. You halt him in front of Amber. "I'm sorry," you blurt out before you can change your mind. "I can't jump in the show Saturday." Dismounting, you hand Sky's reins to Amber.

Before Amber can say anything, you run from the arena. Tears fill your eyes. Not only are you disappointing Amber and the team, you're disappointing yourself. Your fears got the best of you. At least you could have told Amber the truth. Instead, you ran like a chicken.

Halfway to Brightstar House, you slow to a walk. You take off your helmet and wipe your eyes. If you head to your room now, there's a good chance one of the riders will find you there. You're not ready to face them yet. And you certainly aren't ready to explain running away to Amber.

Instead of going to your room, you veer right and hurry into the Star Student Center. Your friend Logan works at the bakery, and something sweet might make you feel better.

"Been riding?" Logan asks as you approach the counter. Her green eyes twinkle beneath her brown bangs.

"Just finished," you tell her. "And I need a pick-me-up," you say, eyeing the cupcakes in the glass case.

"Why do you need a pick-me-up?" Logan asks. She looks at you so kindly that you can't help telling her what happened. After you do, you feel much better.

Logan smiles mischievously and says, "I know *just* what you need."

 Turn to page 56.

"Whoa, whoa!" you holler, trying to get Sky to stop. Your voice sounds shaky and weak. Sky ignores your commands. He gallops across the arena and out the open gate. You hang on to his mane as you bounce in the saddle, still yelling "whoa" in your squeaky voice. Girls and horses scatter from your path.

Sky runs right back into the stable and skids to a halt in front of his stall door. Trembling, you slide from the saddle. Your legs are so wobbly you can hardly stand.

Amber rushes up. "Are you all right?" she asks.

You nod. Your ego is the only thing that's bruised. You acted as if you'd never ridden a horse before! When you catch your breath, you gasp, "Sky needs a better rider."

"You're a good rider," Amber says. "You just need to be more confident."

Boy, do you agree with that.

"I've helped lots of riders gain confidence," Amber says. "We'll start slower next time. Will you give Sky another try?"

After that wild ride, you're not too eager to get on Sky again. But you sure could use help with your confidence.

"Okay," you tell Amber, but your heart is still racing, and you're already dreading "next time."

 Turn to page 51.

Shelby, Devin, and Riley wander off, still talking about the horse show. "Comet's ready to win the Fitting and Showing class," you hear Shelby say. "I've clipped him and brushed him till he shines!"

When your friends are out of earshot, you walk Sky over to Amber. This is your chance to talk to her alone.

"Are you ready to pop a little jump?" Amber asks. "Sky really likes you. I can tell."

You shake your head as you give Sky a pat. "I like him, too," you say sadly. "He's so beautiful, it would be a shame if he didn't compete in the show. But there's no way I'll be confident enough to jump tomorrow, or the next day, or the next." You sigh. "That means I won't be ready to show him Saturday."

Amber's mouth droops. You hate to disappoint her. And what will you tell the other girls? They'll be really disappointed, too.

Then you remember Shelby talking about the Fitting and Showing class. If you and Sky entered, you would only have to lead him into the ring. You could handle that.

You explain your idea to Amber. Her brown eyes light up. "Good idea!" she says. "I could help you get him ready." She holds up her wrist with the cast and adds, "I'm so bummed that I can't ride him."

That gives you an even better idea.

 Turn to page 48.

Heart thumping, you get into jumping position. But you're so scared, your legs clamp against Sky's sides. He rushes forward, leaping too soon. As he soars through the air, you lose your balance. The reins jerk the bit in his mouth.

Sky lands on the other side of the fence, and you bounce out of the saddle like a ball. You hit the ground—hard.

Amber runs over. "Are you all right?" she asks. You sit up, stunned. Amber crouches in front of you, worry creasing her face.

Nothing seems broken, except your confidence. You turn sideways to see if Sky is okay—and to keep Amber from seeing your tears.

Sky is standing right beside you. His reins are dangling, but he seems fine. In fact, he snorts as if to say, *Ready to try that again?*

If you ask Amber to give you a boost back up onto Sky, turn to page 62.

If you decide you're done for the day (but will try again tomorrow), turn to page 54.

If you look for a way out of riding Sky in the show, turn to page 69.

"That's it!" you exclaim.

"What's it?" Amber asks, looking puzzled.

"*You* show Sky in the Fitting and Showing class," you say excitedly. "You only need one hand to lead him into the ring. And the judge is judging both you and Sky."

A hesitant smile lifts Amber's lips. "But your horse has to be perfect to get a ribbon in that class," she says. "With only one good hand, I won't be able to do a great job of grooming, clipping, and braiding him."

"I'd love to help you get Sky ready," you tell Amber. "It will be my way of helping the Innerstar U team."

Amber's smile widens. All this time, you were so worried about yourself that you didn't realize how upset your friend was about not being able to show her favorite horse. "Thank you!" says Amber. She jumps off the fence and gives you a hug. "Let's get started right away. Sky hasn't had a bath in weeks."

You get the hose and help Amber fill a bucket with warm, soapy water. She splashes water on Sky's neck and belly, and he wiggles his upper lip, loving it. After his bath, Amber shows you how to braid his mane. The next day, she shows you how to clip his whiskers and shaggy leg hair. And every day, the two of you use carrots to teach Sky to stand quietly with an alert expression. It's a lot of work, but now that you're not worried about competing, you're having a blast.

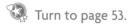 Turn to page 53.

Shelby, Riley, and Devin all start talking at once. The girls are buzzing with excitement, and everyone wants a different game. Finally, Amber puts two fingers in her mouth and whistles.

The girls grow quiet. "Sorry," Riley says. "We got carried away."

"We may not have time to do all of these," Amber says. "Let's vote."

You try to decide which game to vote for. Follow the Leader sounds fun, but your good balance would help in the Egg Race. You've never heard of Zigzag Cones, but it sounds fun, too.

"We need a secret vote," Devin says. "That will be fairer."

You pass out paper and pencils. Each girl writes down her choice. Now you have to make up *your* mind, too.

 If you write down "Egg Race," turn to page 64.

 If you write down "Follow the Leader," turn to page 58.

The next day you sit with Amber by the fountain in Five-Points Plaza. She says that maybe you need a break from riding, and she's right.

"I used to be nervous about showing, too," Amber tells you. "My riding instructor had me practice visualization."

"What's that?" you ask, intrigued.

"Close your eyes," Amber says. "Now picture yourself trotting Sky confidently around the arena."

You let your eyes drift shut. The sound of the fountain's bubbling water is relaxing. You visualize yourself mounted on Sky. He's striding around the arena with his smooth trot. You're posting up and down, moving in time with the beat.

Your eyes pop open. "I see it," you say. "But trotting in an arena is a long way from riding in a show ring."

Amber squeezes your hand. "I know," she says. "And that's okay. I wasn't ready for my first show, either. I was so nervous that I actually got sick."

"Really?" you say. It's hard to picture Amber being that nervous. You're glad she confided in you. You wish you had confided in her earlier. Maybe then you could have worked on your confidence before riding Sky.

"Do you think I'll be ready to show someday?" you ask.

Amber grins. "Let's try visualizing it," she says.

So you do. You picture yourself riding around the ring on show day, with Amber cheering you on. You know that with her support, you *will* be ready—someday soon.

The End

You can't let your teammates down, you decide. Your friends are too important.

"Yeah, Sky and I are ready to win major points," you tell them as you trot over. "He's a dream to ride!"

"You'll be ready for Junior Jumper?" Devin asks.

"Of course," you say confidently, even though a little voice inside you says *not*.

You squelch those negative thoughts. Instead, you picture your teammates congratulating you after a perfect round on Sky.

"If you're going in Junior Jumper, we'd better practice," Amber says. She sets up a jump in the middle of the ring. "We'll start at two foot six inches. You'll be jumping three foot in the show."

You've jumped that high before, you remind yourself. But your heart is thumping so loudly you don't hear Amber's last instructions. You squeeze Sky into a canter. He leaps the fence so high that you barely hang on.

"I said *trot* him," Amber calls. "Otherwise he takes his first fence really big."

Great. Your first jump on Sky, and you get it all wrong.

 If you decide you'd better work harder to squelch those negative thoughts, turn to page 59.

 If your negative thoughts get the better of you, turn to page 60.

Saturday morning, you and Amber are both nervous. You fuss over Sky, making sure every braid in his mane is perfect. Amber combs out his tail one more time.

Now it's time for Amber to get ready. When she comes back into the barn in her Innerstar U riding outfit, you pretend you're speaking into a microphone. "Here's the sensational Amber!" you announce. You both laugh, and suddenly you don't feel quite so nervous.

When it's time for the Fitting and Showing class, Amber leads Sky into the ring along with Shelby and Comet and five other pairs of horses and riders. Sky arches his neck as he parades past the judge. Amber strides confidently beside him, her head tipped proudly.

You're just as proud. Getting ready for the show today was lots of work, but also lots of fun. Maybe next time, you'll be ready to compete yourself. But today is Amber's day to shine with Sky. And when Amber and Sky win first place, you clap and cheer the loudest of all.

The End

The next day, you make up an excuse for not riding Sky. You tell Amber you have too much homework. Then on Thursday, Amber has to work late after class with her lab partner. You're totally relieved. Finally on Friday, you muster up your courage and head to the stables.

Amber is eager to make up for lost time. "Keep your legs steady," she says, "and your seat quiet in the saddle."

All those orders make your head swim, but at least Sky doesn't dump you this time.

Friday night, you toss and turn. Who are you kidding? You're not ready for tomorrow's show. You avoided riding Sky all week. The show is going to be a disaster.

You finally fall asleep, but the next thing you know, Amber is shaking your shoulder and saying, "Wake up. You slept through your alarm!"

Turn to page 61.

"My mane, I mean my hair, could use help," you tell Isabel. A new style won't help you make a decision about riding Sky, but it might take your mind off your problem.

Isabel pulls a handful of ribbons from her dresser drawer. "How about if I braid a red ribbon into your hair?" she asks. "Red is for courage."

"I could use some courage, that's for sure," you admit. As Isabel brushes your hair, you settle back into the chair. The butterflies in your stomach calm down. When Isabel is finished, she holds up a mirror.

The red ribbon winding through your braid does boost your spirits. You only wish it could give you enough confidence to tell Amber yes.

"You need a red bracelet to match your ribbon," Isabel says. "How about a shopping trip to look for more red?"

Before you can answer, Neely dances into Isabel's room. She's singing, as always. "Come fly me to the stars . . ."

You laugh. Neely is always so upbeat and confident.

If you take a minute to ask Neely for advice, turn to page 88.

If you go shopping with Isabel, turn to page 96.

Logan puts on an apron and invites you to follow her into the back kitchen, where a woman is sliding a tray of cupcakes out of an oven.

"Chocolate or vanilla frosting?" Logan asks, holding up an unfrosted cupcake.

"This is a chocolate-sized disaster," you tell her.

"Good choice. It's the baker's secret recipe," Logan adds with a wink.

Sighing, you say, "I just wish there were a recipe for confidence."

"There is!" Logan exclaims. "Take one cupcake," she says as she works. "Spread it with good-friend frosting. Sprinkle it with laughter. Ta-da!" She holds up a chocolate-frosted cupcake topped with colorful sprinkles.

The two of you laugh at the silly recipe. But Logan's right—sharing and laughing with a friend *did* make a difference.

You bite into the sweet, gooey cupcake. It's delicious. Thanking Logan, you head from the bakery. You nearly choke when you spot Amber and Riley coming in the doors of the Student Center. Any minute now, they'll see you. What will you say?

Spinning around, you dash in the opposite direction. You are so not ready to face them.

 Turn to page 63.

"Follow the Leader wins," you say after reading the votes. You nominate Riley to be the first leader, since the game was her idea.

Amber says that she gets to play, too. One of the riding instructors helped her gear up Angel in Western tack so that she'd need only one hand to hold the reins.

Everyone meets in the arena. Sky is excited to see the other horses. He shakes his head and dances in place.

Riley starts off by leading the group in figure eights. Then the horses snake across the ring in an S-shaped pattern. Sky's trot is so smooth that soon you're smiling. The game is a fun way to get used to riding him.

But then Devin, who's behind Riley on Fleet, hollers, "This is too easy! Make it harder!"

"Okay!" Riley yells back. Turning, she aims Rio toward a three-foot fence. Your heart leaps into your throat. You're not ready to jump!

 Turn to page 72.

"Try again!" Riley yells from where she and the others are watching.

You suck in a deep breath. If you're going to help the team on Saturday, you have to be able to jump Sky. *So quit telling yourself that you can't,* you think.

"Trot this time," Amber reminds you.

Sky trots to the jump. Two strides before it, you dig your heels into his sides. That's what you have to do to make sure Angel gets over a fence. Sky takes off. He flies over the jump as if it's four feet high. You lose your balance. Your right foot slips from the stirrup. Thumping hard in the saddle, you jerk Sky in the mouth.

Sky throws up his head. Amber winces.

"Sorry," you apologize. Reality sets in. It's not just your lack of confidence holding you back. You're used to riding Angel, who is a totally different horse. A week just isn't enough time.

"Really sorry," you say again. You slow to a walk in front of Devin, Riley, and Shelby. Amber comes over and gives Sky a pat. You want to tell them you're not a good enough rider for Sky, but you're too embarrassed. "I'm so used to Angel," you say instead.

"Let's try again tomorrow," Amber says. Her expression is so hopeful that you find yourself nodding and saying, "All right."

 Turn to page 66.

"Um, I've got to quit for today," you tell Amber. "I have a test to study for." That's true, but it's a test for your favorite class, so you're bound to ace it.

"Okay," Amber says. "We'll practice again tomorrow."

As you cool down Sky, the word *quitter* keeps flitting through your head. You don't like being a quitter. The only way to do something well—like writing a story or playing the piano—is to practice. That goes for riding, too.

You decide to replace "quitter" with a new motto, like "Practice makes perfect." Okay, maybe not perfect. *No one* is perfect. How about "Practice makes you more confident"? That motto makes sense.

When you get back to the dorm, you e-mail Amber and tell her your new motto. "I'm excited about riding Sky tomorrow," you add. "Meet you at the barn after class!"

 Turn to page 75.

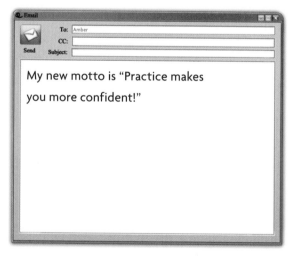

You pop out of bed in a panic. "Hurry and get dressed," Amber says. "I'll groom Sky so that he's ready."

You throw on your riding shirt and pull on your breeches and boots. Grabbing your helmet, you sprint out the door. There's no time for breakfast, so you ignore the hunger pangs in your stomach. Or is that anxiety?

When you reach the barn, Amber has just finished brushing Sky. He looks like a winner. You thank her with an apologetic smile.

"You have time to practice in the warm-up ring," Amber tells you. "But where's your hunt coat?" All the team members are wearing matching blue riding coats. You gasp. In your hurry, you forgot your coat!

 If you borrow one from a teammate, turn to page 67.

 If you dash back to your room, turn to page 68.

You stand up. Your legs are shaking so hard, they wiggle. If you don't get on Sky again right now, you're afraid that you'll chicken out forever.

"Will you give me a leg up?" you ask Amber.

She nods. "You don't have to do this, you know," she says sweetly.

"Yes, I do," you say. You're surprised to hear how strong and determined your voice sounds.

Using her good arm, Amber boosts you into the saddle. Sky dances sideways before you even get your right foot in the stirrup. Amber snaps at him. "Whoa!" she says.

You take a deep breath. *You* should have told Sky "whoa." It's your job to convince Sky that you're in charge. But you can't be in charge if your fear takes over. You need to admit to Amber that you need her help.

"Sky is very different from Angel," you tell Amber. "I'm so used to riding her that I'm not sure I can handle Sky."

Amber smiles. "I understand totally," she says. "When I first started riding Sky, he had me convinced that he was a tiger. But really, he's a kitten."

A kitten? You doubt that.

"The two of you need to learn to trust each other," Amber goes on. "And I know just what to do—but we'll need some help," she says as she turns and jogs out of the ring.

 Turn to page 71.

You duck out the side door of the Student Center. As you lick the chocolate from your fingers, you smile. Logan and her recipe helped give you a little boost, but you need a big boost. You need to create your own recipe for confidence.

You know just where to go for help. The Starlight Library has books on *everything*. The librarian helps you find a few books about building confidence. They look well used. Maybe you're not the only student on campus who's struggling.

After checking out the books, you sigh and settle back into a comfy chair. You prop your helmet on your knee and open the first book.

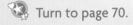 Turn to page 70.

Egg Race wins by one vote. "I won't be able to ride in it because of my cast," says Amber, "but I can be the person who tells you guys what to do!"

Riley jumps up. "I can get eggs and spoons from the Student Center," she says. "I'll meet you guys at the stable."

Twenty minutes later, when everyone is mounted and ready, Amber hands out spoons and eggs. You try to hold yours steady. This is going to be harder than you thought.

"Everyone walk," Amber announces.

You steer Sky with one hand on the reins. Your gaze is glued to the egg.

"Trot!" Amber calls. *Uh-oh.* You squeeze your heels into Sky's sides. He breaks into a smooth trot. You post—up and down—the egg jiggling each time you move.

"Argh!" Devin hollers. "Hey, Riley, I thought you said these were hard-boiled." She leans over to brush egg yolk from her pant leg.

"Oops," says Riley, giggling. A second later, her egg has fallen, too. Now only Shelby and you are left.

"Canter," Amber says.

Sky moves smoothly into the canter, as if he wants to win as much as you do. You hear a commotion behind you, and Shelby starts laughing. You and Sky won! If only you could be a winner in the show ring, too. Maybe it's time to confide in the team about your worries.

 Turn to page 87.

"I'll, uh, give Sky a bath," you tell Amber as you dismount. You watch your friend leave, wishing you had the courage to tell her you can't do this. Sighing, you lead Sky from the ring. Your head's hanging. Riley meets you at the gate and walks to the stable with you.

"Hey, don't look so sad. You and Sky didn't do badly for the first time," Riley says brightly.

"Are you kidding? It's a wonder I didn't fall off," you scoff. "There's no way I can jump Sky on Saturday."

"Don't say that," Riley says soothingly. "Maybe this was just a bad day. Everyone has them. I'm kind of having one, too."

You glance up. "Really?" you say.

Riley nods. "Rio was playing out in the pasture this morning," she begins, "and another horse kicked him. The instructor said he can't compete in the show. I'm going to ride Lollipop in the Walk, Trot, Canter class instead."

Halting Sky, you turn to stare at Riley. *That's it!* You think excitedly. *That's the solution to my problem!* You hurry into the stable to find Amber.

 If the solution is riding Sky in a Walk, Trot, Canter class instead of jumping, turn to page 74.

If the solution is matching Riley and Sky together, turn to page 76.

Shelby comes running up the aisle, holding out her hunt coat. "I heard what happened," she says breathlessly. "Wear mine. That'll give you time to warm up Sky."

Shelby is shorter than you. Will the coat fit?

"Hurry," Amber says as she puts the saddle on Sky. "Your class is next."

There's no time to get your own coat now. "Thanks, Shelby," you say. You slip on the coat. It's so small, you can button only one button.

Amber gives you a leg up into the saddle and checks the girth—the strap around Sky's belly. You can't look her in the eyes. You're too embarrassed by all the mistakes you've made. Hopefully, since you have time before the class to practice on Sky, everything will be okay.

At least that's what you tell yourself as you ride Sky into the warm-up ring. Several other riders are schooling their horses for the Junior Jumper class. One is wearing Hillside's dark blue hunt coat. She and her horse fly over the school-ing fence in perfect form.

She'll be tough competition, but that's not what you're thinking about as you trot Sky around the ring. You're too busy sucking in your stomach. Shelby's coat is so tight, you can barely breathe.

"Junior Jumper class," the announcer calls. Your heart drops. You'd better practice at least one jump before they call your number.

 Turn to page 112.

"Run back and get your coat," Amber says, making shooing motions with her hand. "Riley can help me tack up Sky."

You race to Brightstar House as quickly as you can, clomping awkwardly along the path in your new riding boots. By the time you reach your room, you feel light-headed. Now you wish you'd taken the time to eat some breakfast, at least a granola bar.

You dart into your walk-in closet, glancing high and low. Where's your hunt coat?

Finally you find it, still in the shopping bag. Tucking the coat under your arm, you race back to the stables. By the time you get there, you feel a blister forming on your heel. Amber is holding Sky by the show ring. She looks relieved to see you. As you hurry toward her, you put on your coat.

"You're next!" Amber says. She boosts you into the saddle.

"What about warming up Sky?" you ask as you snap on your helmet strap.

Amber shakes her head. "There's no time," she says.

Sky begins pawing. Amber bites her lip. Your pulse is beating a mile a minute. Both of you know that skipping the warm-up is a recipe for disaster.

"Good luck," Amber whispers.

You force a smile. "Thanks," you say. "I'll need it."

 Turn to page 78.

"I might have sprained my ankle," you tell Amber.

"Let me help you," she says. She holds out her hand and pulls you to your feet. Your ankle isn't sprained, but it's the only excuse you can think of to get out of riding Sky.

"Can you put weight on it?" Amber asks.

"Yeah. It's just a little sore. Sorry," you mumble.

"Don't worry," Amber says. "I know how you feel. Go get your ankle checked at the health center."

"Thanks," you say. You hobble from the ring. You hate fibbing to Amber, but what else can you say? That you can't control Sky? That you're too chicken to ride him?

That night, you e-mail Amber. You tell her that you're not supposed to put weight on your ankle for a week. (By then, you figure, the show will be over.)

Amber is totally understanding. She says it's okay. Only it's not okay. You'd rather fake a sprained ankle than admit the truth to Amber. You're so disappointed in yourself!

Show day finds you alone in your room while the other girls are cheering on the Innerstar U team. You're too embarrassed to even think about joining them.

The End

An hour later, you're still reading the first book. Building confidence takes time, you realize—definitely more than a week, which is all the time you have to prepare for the show.

Closing the book, you look out the window. The sun is setting over campus. There's a soft golden glow. As you watch the sun slowly disappear behind the Star Student Center, a recipe forms in your mind.

You smile. You may not be ready for Saturday's show. But if you follow your recipe, you might have the confidence to tackle the next one.

The End

Recipe for confidence

Take one cup of "you can do it!"
Add one inspiring motto.
Stir in a heaping cup of positive thinking.
Add a tablespoon of deep breathing.
Mix in practice and preparation.
Sprinkle on courage to taste.
Bake slowly and enjoy with good friends.

Amber returns with an instructor, who carries a long flat rope called a lunge line. She attaches the lunge line to the bit rings on either side of Sky's bridle.

"What are we going to do?" you ask curiously.

"I'm going to lunge Sky in a circle," the instructor says. "You're going to ride him with no reins."

"No reins?" you exclaim. You swallow hard.

"It helps your balance," Amber explains. "And it helps you communicate with Sky without using your reins."

The instructor takes the reins from you and makes a knot in them. "Go ahead and get Sky walking," she says.

You squeeze Sky's sides with your calves. He strides off quickly in a circle. You lurch forward. It feels odd riding without the reins.

"Put your arms out to help you balance," the instructor suggests. You raise your arms at your sides, which helps.

"Good. Remember to breathe," the instructor says.

You let out your breath. The sun feels warm on your face. Sky's gaits are smooth. You slowly ease into them.

"Great job!" Amber says when you're done.

Leaning forward, you stroke Sky's neck. He was a good partner, and you were brave, too. You tried something new, and it worked!

 Turn to page 79.

Riley and Rio take the jump perfectly, with Devin close behind. Your stomach is doing flip-flops. You've jumped Angel over three foot before, but you've never jumped Sky.

"I'm out!" Amber calls as she trots Angel to the other side of the ring. She can't jump in a Western saddle.

You want to holler, "I'm out, too!" But you force yourself to swallow your fear. As you near the jump, you pretend you're riding Angel—good old reliable Angel. Sky arcs over the rails beautifully. When he lands, he gives a little buck of joy. You grin. That was fun!

The team game is working for you. It's helping you relax and enjoy riding a new horse.

After the game, you trot Sky over to Amber. You tell her that with practice, you'll be ready to ride Sky in the show.

"Great!" says Amber. "Tomorrow, I'll give you a real jumping lesson on Sky."

Turn to page 75.

"I want to ride Sky in the competition," you tell Amber. "But I'm not ready for jumping. How about if we switch to a Walk, Trot, Canter class?"

"But Sky's one of our best jumpers," Amber says. "And you're a good jumper, too. And we can practice every day."

"That might help my form," you say, "but it won't help . . ." You hesitate, and then you take a deep breath and continue. "It won't help my confidence."

Amber looks at you for a long moment and then smiles. "Okay," she says. "I'll tell the instructor to enter you in Walk, Trot, Canter. Tomorrow, we'll start practicing for it."

That sounds like a great idea to you.

The day of the show, all eyes are on you as you canter Sky around the ring. The judge is checking you out as he writes on his clipboard. Amber, Devin, and Shelby are cheering from the railing.

Sky's head is slightly tucked. His tail flows behind him. His dapples glisten.

You sit lightly in the saddle and move evenly to Sky's beat. All week, Amber worked with you and Sky, preparing you for the Walk, Trot, Canter class. Your practice has paid off. Riding Sky feels like a dream, and your spirits soar.

Your confidence is soaring, too. So when the announcer calls that first place in the Walk, Trot, Canter class goes to you and Silver Sky, you know that the two of you deserve it!

The End

The next day, you feel more nervous than excited about your lesson. You listen carefully to Amber. You trot Sky over the first jump, a small crossbar. He clears it smoothly.

"Super!" Amber calls. "Let's try a simple line of jumps." She points to two obstacles in a row. One is a small gate. The other is a box of brush. Your pulse begins to race.

Sky jumps the obstacles easily, and you manage to stay on him. Your form is a little shaky, but with practice, you'll get better.

"Hi, guys," Devin calls as she rides into the arena on Fleet. Her young Thoroughbred is gorgeous and talented. You know that the team hopes the pair will win lots of points at the show.

You and Amber call hello. Then Amber compliments you on the jump. "That was great," she says. "By Saturday, you and Sky should be ready for Junior Jumper."

Your throat tightens. Junior Jumper sounds scary.

"You and Devin are entered in the same class," adds Amber.

"We are?" you blurt. Eek! Fleet can jump every obstacle in the arena—and make it look easy.

 Turn to page 77.

"Riley, you should ride Sky!" you exclaim.

Riley looks puzzled. "I thought you were riding Sky," she says.

"I was, but Sky and I just aren't meshing," you explain. "He's so different from Angel. But Sky and Rio are similar. I think you two would be great together."

Riley smiles. "You think so?" she says. "I love to jump. I was so disappointed when Rio got kicked."

"Come on, let's go find Amber," you say excitedly. Leading Sky, you head down the aisle of the barn. Amber is helping Shelby clip Comet in one of the stalls. You explain your idea to Amber.

"But don't you want to ride Sky?" Amber asks you.

"I did," you say. "But after riding Sky, I realized I wasn't the best rider for him. I want Innerstar U to win, and Riley can help you guys do that."

Amber looks from you to Riley and then back again. "Okay, then," she finally says with a smile. "Do you want to try him out tomorrow, Riley?"

"Yes!" Riley says. She slaps palms with Amber and then with you. You're glad that she's so excited. And you have to admit, you're totally relieved that you don't have to ride Sky.

The next day, Riley rides Sky over a small practice course while the rest of the team watches. Riley and Sky are a perfect match!

 Turn to page 118.

You watch as Devin rides Fleet over a tight "in and out." Fleet jumps over a fence, takes one stride, and immediately clears a second fence. You're totally impressed.

"Nice!" you say as Devin trots over to you and Amber.

"Thanks," Devin says. She halts her horse. "I hear we're entered in the same class."

"Uh, yeah," you say. "Though it seems you and Fleet should be in a harder class."

Devin shrugs. "He's still young," she says. "This is only his first year showing."

That doesn't make you feel any better.

"Well, good luck Saturday," Devin says. But as she turns Fleet away, you hear her mutter, "You're going to need it."

"Don't listen to her," Amber says quickly. "By Saturday, you'll be ready to give her some good competition."

If you believe Devin is right, turn to page 82.

If you believe Amber—that you and Sky will be ready—turn to page 84.

If you ask your teammates for advice, turn to page 87.

You steer Sky toward the in-gate, wishing you were on the moon, in China, anywhere but at this show.

Then Riley dashes up. "Amber told me you and Sky didn't get to warm up," she says. "Can I give you a tip?"

"Please do," you say.

Riley touches your arm. "I bet you're tense," she says. "Remember that Sky's a pro. If you relax, he'll be fine."

You roll your eyes. "After this crazy week, there's no way I can relax," you say.

"You can," Riley insists. "I learned some great yoga techniques that I use before competing."

The horse before you is just finishing up its round. Riley had better hurry if she's going to help you relax.

She holds onto Sky's rein. "Close your eyes," she says in a soft voice. "Inhale deeply, count to five, and then exhale."

You give it a try. You breathe in and then out. You take another deep breath, and then another. Slowly, the knot in your shoulders loosens. Your anxiety starts to disappear. Calm drifts over you—until you hear a panicky voice holler, "You forgot to memorize the jump course!"

 Turn to page 86.

By Friday, you and Sky are meshing. You're taking those jumps like pros. You're even dreaming about winning a ribbon in tomorrow's competition.

Just before dinner, Riley comes into your room. She's modeling her riding outfit for the show. "Ta-da!" she says. "What do you think?"

"Wow!" you gush. "You look like a winner." Then you give yourself a mental slap on the forehead. You've been so busy riding all week, you forgot about your own outfit.

Riley helps you rummage through your walk-in closet. In the back, you find your breeches, shirt, tall black boots, and hunt coat. You wore them for the last show—but that was months ago. Since then, you've had a growth spurt.

You try on your outfit.

"Uh, wow?" Riley says. Her pained expression says it all—you look ridiculous.

Your shirtsleeves are too short, and you can barely button your breeches. Even your boots are a little too small. You give Riley an anguished look as you change back into your jeans. "What am I going to do?" you wail.

 Turn to page 104.

That afternoon, Amber helps you tack up Sky. This time, you use your firm voice. You don't let him push you around.

You and Shelby practice in the ring together, pretending it's a show. Shelby hollers, "You and Sky look great together! He's gorgeous, and the perfect size for you."

"Thanks," you say. Shelby's going to be a great support buddy, you think. "You and Comet look good, too," you call to her.

Shelby frowns and says, "Yeah, until we start cantering. Then I look like a sack of potatoes."

You giggle, trying to picture it. But when Shelby starts cantering Comet, you realize she's sort of right about the potatoes. Fortunately, you know just how to help her.

"When Comet starts to canter, your legs move too far forward," you explain. Helping Shelby takes your mind off your worries. You relax in the saddle and have such a good ride with Sky that you know "yes" was the right decision.

Turn to page 83.

You clutch your stomach. Devin's right. You barely got Sky over two small jumps. There's no way you'll be ready for Saturday's show.

"Amber, I don't feel so hot," you say. "Can you cool down Sky for me?"

"Of course," says Amber. She looks at you with concern, but you can't bring yourself to tell her why your stomach is in knots. Your confidence failed you—in a big way.

By the time you make it back to your room, your head hurts. You peel off your riding clothes and climb into bed.

The next morning, you're still not feeling well. Did you catch the bug that's going around the dorm? Or are your negative thoughts making you sick? Either way, you can't ride Sky. You crawl out of bed and e-mail Amber.

Sorry about yesterday, you write. *Still sick today. I won't be ready to ride Sky in the show.*

You pause. The word *quitter* pops into your head. You bet that's what Amber will be thinking. At least, that's what you're thinking about yourself.

No wonder you're feeling sick. You swallow a wave of misery and climb back into bed.

The End

You and Shelby practice all week. Before you know it, it's the day of the competition. Shelby and Comet compete first in a Walk, Trot, Canter class.

You and your teammates watch from the railing. When Shelby trots past, you give her a thumbs-up. The pair isn't the flashiest, but Shelby is beaming with confidence.

The announcer calls, "Canter, all canter, please." You hold your breath. Comet breaks into a smooth canter. Shelby sits quietly in the saddle, moving rhythmically with his stride. Your exercises and her practice paid off!

"Go, Shelby!" you shout. Cheering for your friend takes the focus off your own jitters—and, wow, are you nervous about your Jumping class. This is your first show since that horrible day when you fell off.

The horses line up in the middle of the ring. Shelby gives you a nervous smile. The judge hands out the first, second, and third place ribbons. Your heart sinks. Will your friend place at all?

"In fourth place is Shelby on Comet," the announcer calls. Shelby rides forward and accepts a white ribbon.

"Congratulations!" you cry as you meet her at the exit gate. She's grinning from ear to ear.

"Your class is coming up," Shelby tells you. "Then it will be your turn to shine."

She's right. It's time to prove that you and Sky can do this, too.

 Turn to page 85.

You try to shake off Devin's comment. "Let's practice some more," you say with determination.

"That's the spirit," says Amber. She walks over to the "in and out." She lowers the rails on both fences. You gulp.

"I've never jumped an 'in and out' before," you admit.

"But Sky has," says Amber. "It'll be a piece of cake."

It's *not* a piece of cake. You have to grab Sky's mane to hang on over each fence. But Amber's right—Sky handles it like a pro. By the time your lesson is over, you're feeling more confident about riding him. But enough to compete against Devin and Fleet? It's time to tell Amber the truth.

You dismount and lead Sky over to her. "Amber, I had fun riding Sky today," you begin. "And I do want to show Saturday. But there's no way I'll be confident enough to beat Devin. I'll probably be so nervous, I won't beat anyone. That won't help the team."

For a moment, Amber is silent. You flush. What if she doesn't understand? Maybe you should have kept your doubts to yourself.

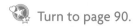 Turn to page 90.

When the announcer calls your number, your heart jumps. Shelby meets you at the in-gate. She gives your hand a squeeze. "Remember," she tells you, "you're already a winner for braving the show. Now go in there and do your best."

Shelby's words give you a boost. Then Amber, Riley, and Devin hurry over. "Hey, teammate," they chorus, "we're rooting for you!" Their cheers send you into the ring with a smile.

Sky strides into the ring, his ears flicking at the sights. You talk quietly to him, hoping to settle him—and yourself. "We can do this," you tell Sky. "Shelby has confidence in me. Amber has confidence in you, and so do I. Let's show them, okay?"

Turn to page 103.

You're a winner for braving the show.

Your eyes fly open. Amber is running across the show grounds, holding a sheet of paper. In all the rushing around this morning, you never walked the course. The announcer is about to call your number. You won't know what order to jump the fences in!

"You forgot to memorize the course?" Riley asks, forgetting she's supposed to be helping you calm down.

Amber waves the sheet as she gets closer. Sky shies at the flapping paper, knocking into the horse next to him. You slip sideways. Grabbing his mane, you manage to stay in the saddle. But now Sky is as rattled as you are.

"You have one minute," Amber gasps. She hands you the sheet, but it's all arrows and lines.

Sky bobs his head nervously. The knot tightens in your shoulders. You glance from the sheet to the announcer and back again. You've got to do something, or this will be a total disaster!

If you ask Amber to help you memorize the course, turn to page 94.

If you use that minute to practice Riley's calming techniques, turn to page 93.

"I love riding Sky," you admit to your friends when you're back in the stable. "It's showing I don't like. In my last show, the horse refused, and I fell off."

"Did you fall on top of the judge?" Devin asks, laughing. Riley, Amber, and Shelby laugh, too. Are they making fun of you?

"We're not laughing *at* you," Shelby says gently. "We're laughing with you. All of us have crazy horse show stories."

"During my last show, Rio almost ran over the judge," Riley says. "The judge told me to leave the ring and never come back."

"During a Walk, Trot, Canter class, Comet ducked out of the gate," Shelby says. "He galloped all the way back to the horse van."

Even Devin has a tale to tell. Pretty soon, you're laughing, too.

"So how do all of you keep from getting scared before the show?" you ask.

"Focus on your horse. Help him do his best," Shelby suggests.

"Don't even think about the other riders," Riley adds.

"And definitely don't worry about the judge," Amber says. "Unless you're about to run over him."

That starts you all laughing again. You're so glad you talked to the team. You're already feeling more confident.

 Turn to page 91.

"When I have to make a hard decision, I make a list," Neely tells you. She pulls a notepad from her backpack. "Let's write down all the things you love to do. That will help you make up your mind."

You start to list your favorite things, such as riding horses, reading, helping friends, listening to music, and going to concerts. When you finish the list, you notice that jumping in a horse show is not on it. But helping friends is on it. And riding Sky would be helping out Amber and the team. You sigh.

"I see that going to concerts is on your list," Neely says. "Did you know that the band the Strawberries is playing at Innerstar U?"

"I *love* the Strawberries!" you and Isabel exclaim together.

"I've got two extra tickets for helping out at the ticket booth," Neely says. "The concert's Saturday afternoon."

Saturday afternoon! That's the same day as the horse show.

The Strawberries is your favorite group. Your decision just got more complicated.

If you decide to go to the concert with Neely and Isabel, turn to page 95.

If you decide to ride Silver Sky to help Amber and the team, turn to page 99.

Then Amber gives you a huge smile. "Boy, do you have horse show jitters," she says. "Don't think so much about winning. Instead, focus on having fun."

Fun? To you, fun is eating a hot fudge sundae and dancing to the band the Strawberries.

"Don't let Devin get to you," Amber continues. "All she thinks about is winning. That doesn't mean you have to."

"But we're on the same team," you say. "We should be working together to earn points."

"You're right about that," Amber says. She pauses and then says, "Let's talk to the team tonight. Maybe we *all* need to work on having more fun together."

 Turn to page 110.

Don't think about winning. Focus on having fun.

INNERSTAR UNIVERSITY

Your confidence doesn't last long. Saturday morning, you learn that there are six schools competing in the show. As you watch some of the jumping classes, you realize how good the riders are—much better than you, that's for sure. Plus, the other Innerstar U team members are so busy worrying about their classes that you don't feel the team bond you felt a few days ago.

Your spirits sink even lower when you ride Sky into the warm-up ring. A dozen other riders are warming up. You recognize the school colors of Hillside and Annandale. Devin and Fleet are practicing over a small fence, too. The duo looks perfect. All these riders will be competing against you.

You remind yourself that Sky is beautiful and a great jumper. He has a good chance if you keep your cool. After warming up at a trot, you canter him toward the practice jump. You forget Amber's advice to keep him slow and steady. Sky clears the jump by two feet. You plop down awkwardly in the saddle, losing your stirrups.

Devin trots by. "Having trouble?" she asks with a smug smile. She knows you don't have a chance.

 Turn to page 107.

"I've got an idea," Amber says. "The team needs a manager, someone to help clean tack, horses, and the barn. I can't do it, not with only one arm."

"I've got a better idea," you say. "Let's do the job *together*."

Amber's eyes widen happily. "Yes!" she says.

You and Amber work hard to get the team ready for the show. You enjoy helping your friend—and the team. And by show day, the stable, tack, and horses gleam.

Saturday morning, you and Amber are raking out stalls when a man strolls into the barn. It's the top judge! He walks around the horses and makes a few marks on his clipboard. When he leaves, you let out your breath.

There's no time to worry, though. The announcer calls for Devin's class to start, and Riley is next. Both girls need your help. All you can do is hope your hard work pays off.

At the end of the show, the announcer calls the results of the surprise inspection. Innerstar U won the highest marks! You and Amber jump up and down with excitement. Devin, Riley, and Shelby crowd around you, cheering.

Okay, so you might have had more fun riding today. Maybe by the next show, you'll be ready. Still, with the help of your teammates, you came up with an idea that worked for everyone. That deserves a rousing cheer!

The End

"There's no time," you tell Amber, pushing away the course map. Instead of cramming to memorize the course, you close your eyes and take a few more deep breaths. Your heart stops racing, and Sky seems to settle down a bit, too.

"Number twelve riding Silver Sky into the ring, please," the announcer calls.

"Twice around the outside and down the middle," Amber says quickly.

You try to memorize her words as you trot Sky into the ring. Riley's tricks worked. Sky is calmer and listening to your signals, and you're more focused, too.

"Once around and down the middle," you repeat to yourself. You point Sky to the first jump. He sails over it and the next three beautifully. Your confidence is growing as you point him down the middle.

"Number twelve, off course," the announcer says. "Please leave the ring."

Startled, you slow Sky to a trot. Off course? Did the judge make a mistake? Then you realize that *you* were the one who made the mistake. Not memorizing the course cost the team points. You're so ashamed, you ride Sky straight back to the stables. You untack him and put him in the stall.

If you rush off so that you don't have to face Amber, turn to page 108.

If you decide you have to face the team, turn to page 116.

"Help me memorize the course," you plead with Amber. She holds up the sheet so that you can see it. "There are two jumps on each side of the ring," she says. "And one jump in the middle. You need to go twice around, clockwise, down the middle, and up the far side counterclockwise."

You repeat Amber's instructions to yourself. When your name blasts from the intercom, you yelp in surprise.

"You can do it!" Riley says, giving you a thumbs-up.

As you guide Sky into the ring, he breaks into a nervous trot. At the same time, your stomach flutters with anxiety. "Easy, Sky," you say. "We can do this."

Sky doesn't listen. He breaks into a canter and charges the first two fences. Luckily, he clears them. You tilt your head toward the second line of two fences. Tightening your grip, you try to get Sky to slow down. Instead, he bounds ahead, knocking down two rails.

You're out of the ribbons, you think. But Sky hasn't refused, and you're staying on. Taking a few deep breaths as Riley suggested helps you sit quieter in the saddle. You relax your grip on the reins. Sky relaxes, too, and quits rushing, and you finish the rest of the course with no faults.

 Turn to page 100.

You drag your feet all the way back to Rising Star Stables. You find Amber in the barn, brushing Sky's tail.

"I've made a decision," you tell Amber. You can barely get the words out. "I think Sky is beautiful, but I can't ride him in the show."

Amber tries to hide her disappointment with a smile. "Thanks for letting me know," she says softly.

You tell her that you're sorry, but you know that "sorry" won't help Amber or the team.

Still, your steps feel lighter as you jog back to the dorm. Your butterflies of worry slowly disappear. You're just so relieved that you don't have to ride in the show.

The day of the concert, you, Neely, and Isabel all sport berry-red ribbons in your hair. The Strawberries run onto stage singing their most popular song. You scream along with every other girl in the audience. You know the lyrics by heart: "Best friends . . . do things for each other. Best friends . . . stand by you forever."

As you think about the words, your throat tightens. The song reminds you that you weren't a good friend to Amber, and you let Devin, Riley, and Shelby down, too. Your guilt hangs heavy throughout the rest of the song.

You wish you had handled your decision better. At least you could have helped Amber find another rider for Sky. If you had, then today at the concert, you'd be having a lot more fun.

The End

"If red gives you courage, then I want to be decked out in it," you tell Isabel. "From head to toe. Let's go shopping!"

The Shopping Square is always busy. Girls duck in and out of shops on the cobblestone street. In one boutique, you find the perfect red hat. You toss it to Isabel. "How's this?" you ask her.

"That will definitely give a girl courage," Isabel says. She plunks the hat on her head and then drapes a red cape over your shoulders.

You giggle. "A cape didn't help Little Red Riding Hood," you protest.

Next you try on sparkly red shoes. "I feel like Dorothy in *The Wizard of Oz*," you say.

"Look!" Isabel waves for you to join her at a jewelry rack. Pretty soon, she has beads strung around her neck and wrists. "Here's one for you," she says, pointing to a ruby-red bracelet.

"I could hide it under the sleeve of my hunt coat!" you exclaim. You try on the bracelet. It's a perfect fit. You buy the bracelet, and Isabel buys the red hat.

As you walk back to Brightstar House, your step seems lighter. Maybe it's the red bracelet around your wrist, or maybe it was the fun afternoon with Isabel, but your fears seem to have melted away.

 Turn to page 102.

You nod at Amber's words, but your attention is still on Devin. She's cantering Fleet, looking way too perfect.

"You're next in the ring," Amber says.

You jerk upright in the saddle. "I am?" you squawk. You hurry Sky into the show ring.

The judge holds a clipboard in his hand, and his eyes are fixed on you. Sweat runs down your forehead. Your fingers clutch the reins. Sky canters too fast to the first fence. When you pull back to slow him down, he fights you. He sails too high over the first two jumps.

You glance at the judge. He's still writing. About what? Your terrible riding? Sky feels your attention wander. Too late, you feel his hesitation. He skids to a halt in front of the third jump.

The refusal jolts you into action. Turning Sky, you aim him again at the jump. This time you focus on him and the jump. "You can do it," you tell him. He easily finishes the round.

Tears fill your eyes as you leave the ring. A refusal knocks you out of the ribbons. You can't believe it happened to you again! But that's not really true. You know *exactly* why it happened again. You did everything wrong. You ignored your friends' advice. You took your focus off Sky.

You're so disappointed. Next time, you tell yourself, you'll worry less about everyone else and more about doing your best—and helping your horse do his best, too.

The End

"Thanks, Neely, but I can't go to the concert," you tell her. "Your list helped me decide. I love to ride, and I love to help friends. If I ride Sky in the show, I'll be doing both."

"I understand," Neely says sweetly. She pauses and then adds, "You could also try what I do whenever I perform onstage. Act confident, and you'll feel more confident." Tipping her head high, she sashays around the room. She looks like a celebrity doing a red-carpet walk.

As you walk back to the stable, you practice your red-carpet walk. It helps you feel more confident, but you still don't feel ready to enter a Jumper class. There must be another way to help out the team.

Turn to page 101.

Act confident, and you'll feel more confident.

"Good job, Sky!" you say, bending to pat his sweaty neck. You knocked down two rails, so there's no way you'll win points for the team. But you and Sky made it around the course despite the morning's craziness.

"I'm sorry I wasn't a better partner for you," you tell Sky. You dismount and give him a hug. It wasn't Sky's fault that he knocked down the rails. If you had spent this week practicing instead of feeling scared, you and Sky might have had a clean round.

That realization gives you a boost of confidence—and an idea. You wave to Amber, who's headed your way.

"Sky did super," you tell her. "Let's enter him in a second class. I'll be sure to walk the course, warm him up, and give him the best ride I can."

Amber agrees. *This time,* you vow, *I'll get it right.*

The End

You find Amber in the barn, scrubbing out a bucket. "I've made my decision," you say, smiling. "I'll do it."

"Yippee!" Amber shouts, dropping her sponge.

"Wait," you say, catching her arm. "Um, I'll ride in the show, but not in a jumping class."

"Why not?" asks Amber, clearly confused. "Sky's one of the best jumpers in the barn."

"He is, but I'm not," you admit.

Amber seems surprised by that. "But you jump Angel all the time," she says.

"On the *trail*," you explain. "Couldn't we enter Sky in another class? Something not quite so . . . scary?" There, you finally said it.

"I don't know," Amber says. She frowns as she thinks it through. You can tell she wants to help you with this. You wonder why you waited so long to tell her how you felt.

"I don't know about a different class," Amber says. "The team needs Sky to win points in one of the more advanced classes."

Amber sees the disappointment in your face. "Don't worry," she says kindly. "We'll figure out something."

⭐ If you and Amber decide to enter Sky in a different advanced class, turn to page 114.

⭐ If you and Amber decide that you can help the team in another way, turn to page 92.

The next day, you wear your red bracelet when you tell Amber that you'll ride in the show. And you wear it every day while you practice riding Sky. It's your good luck charm, for sure. Isabel helps, too, by cheering you on.

"You and Sky look like something out of a fairy tale," she says on Friday. "Like a princess on her steed."

That evening, after you brush out Sky's tail and mane, he *does* look fit for a princess. Still, when you think about the Junior Jumper class, your stomach knots. What happens if Sky refuses a fence? You won't be a princess anymore.

Sighing, you touch the red beads. You know they aren't really magic, yet somehow they've helped you believe in yourself all week. You hope they will work tomorrow, too.

The next morning, you ride Sky proudly into the show ring. His mane and tail are braided with red yarn. Isabel is in the stands in her funny red hat. You have on your red bracelet, too. When you touch the beads, you feel a boost of confidence. You don't know if you'll take home a ribbon, but you already feel like a winner, and now you know you can handle whatever comes your way.

The End

Trotting, you head to the first jump. Sky breaks into a canter and clears it and the second fence easily. You breathe a sigh of relief as he makes it all the way around the course twice. Sky isn't going to refuse. You won't fall off.

You turn him sharply to head down the middle. So far, he's jumped perfectly. If you and Sky have a clear round, you could win a blue or red ribbon—and major points for the team!

Then Sky slips in the grass. He meets the first fence down the middle—a gate—at an angle. He hits the top of the gate, takes two strides, and sails over the last fence. His right hind hoof cracks loudly on the top rail. It crashes to the ground behind you.

Your heart sinks. No ribbon. No points. You're sure that your friends will be disappointed.

You couldn't be more wrong. Shelby and Amber greet you with huge smiles. "Terrific round!" Amber praises. "You rode him like a champ."

"Atta way, support buddy," says Shelby, giving you a high five. Riley and Devin gather round you and Sky, too.

Okay, so you won't win a ribbon, but you won something even better: good friends and confidence. Your teammates believed in you, and now you believe in yourself, too.

The End

Riley pushes you out the door. "First things first," she says. "You can figure it out over dinner."

"I don't have time to eat," you tell her, but Isabel is walking down the hall toward you. She hooks your elbow with hers. "Lasagna tonight. Your fave," she says as she propels you down the hall.

Lasagna *is* one of your favorites, and your stomach is growling with hunger. Laughing, you head down the hall with Isabel. You'll worry about that too-small riding outfit after dinner.

As soon as dinner is over, you *do* start to worry. You skip dessert and rush back to your room. How are you going to pull together an outfit in such a short time? When you burst through the door to your room, you jump backward.

"Surprise!" voices sing out. Riley and Shelby are in the middle of your room, holding up an Innerstar U hunt coat and tan breeches. Even Devin is squatting on the floor next to them, holding up a pair of tall black boots. "I think they're just your size," she says with a genuine smile.

You blink back tears. "You guys are the best," you say. "I'm so glad I decided to ride for the team."

"We're glad, too," Riley says. "Now hurry up and try everything on!"

 Turn to page 109.

Amber's totally right, you realize. If you let your anger at Devin take over, you won't be the best rider for Sky. You take a deep breath and try to focus on Sky. He seems jittery, and no wonder. You treated him as if he were the problem.

"I'm going to try that warm-up fence again," you tell Amber. This time, you keep a cool head. Sky floats over the fence. You stroke his neck. "Good boy," you murmur.

You hear the announcer call your number. "Calm and steady," you whisper to Sky. As you steer him around the course, you keep your gaze between his ears. You focus your attention on each jump. Sky meets one fence too closely and knocks down a rail. But it doesn't rattle you, and he finishes the rest of the course with no faults.

Devin and Fleet ride next. They have a clear round. Devin wins a blue ribbon—and ten points for the team. You're riding Sky over to congratulate Devin when the announcer calls your name. Fifth place! You trot Sky into the ring, amazed. The judge hands you a pink ribbon.

When you ride out, Shelby, Amber, and Riley rush over to greet you. "Super job!" Amber says.

"But we knocked down a rail," you say.

"Most of the other horses did, too," Riley explains. "It was a tough course, but you earned three points!"

You're proud of yourself, and you're proud of Sky. You both did your best, but you couldn't have done it without the support of your friends.

The End

Devin's attitude makes you mad. She's your teammate. Why isn't she supporting you?

Red-faced with embarrassment, you halt Sky. You find your stirrups. The other riders warming up in the ring all seem to be staring at you.

"Don't think about the other riders," you remember Riley saying.

"Focus on your horse. Help him do his best," says Shelby's voice in your head. Good advice, only you're doing just the opposite!

Still steamed at Devin, you rein Sky toward the gate. You want out of that warm-up ring.

"Everything okay?" Amber asks as you ride through the gate.

"Fine," you say. "I just wish Devin weren't so . . . so . . ."

"Overconfident?" Amber guesses. She pats Sky's neck. "Just focus on Sky," she says. "He can do it. Have confidence in *him*."

 If you watch Devin warm up, turn to page 98.

 If you try to focus on Sky, turn to page 106.

You sneak from the stable, your helmet pulled low. Amber spots you anyway.

"Wait!" she calls as she runs up to you. Reluctantly, you stop. Amber's fists are propped on her hips. She's frowning. "Aren't you forgetting something?" she asks.

"Umm, I—I'm sorry about messing up the course?" you stammer.

"You forgot about Sky," says Amber. "You tossed him in the stall without cooling him down. He could get sick."

Your jaw drops. Now you're upset with yourself. You were so worried about what your friends would think that you forgot about your horse. "I'm sorry, Amber," you say sincerely. "I was so freaked out that all I could think of was disappearing. You know I'd never hurt Sky on purpose."

Amber's eyes soften. "I know," she says. "But hurt pride should never come before your horse. Right?"

"Right," you say sadly. You hurry back into the barn. You need to show Amber that you can do something right.

 Turn to page 119.

Saturday morning, you show up at the stables in your "new" riding outfit. Everything fits perfectly. Sky looks terrific, too, with his braided mane and glossy coat.

You feel a rush of confidence as you enter the ring. You expertly steer Sky around the course. He responds to your leg aids and your touch on the reins. Sure, your heart is beating like a drum. But the confidence-building exercises and practice have paid off. The two of you are a true team as you canter around the jump course.

On the last obstacle, Sky takes off too soon. He hits the top rail with a hind foot. You can hear the pole crash to the ground, but you don't let it bother you. "Great job," you tell Sky as you trot out the exit gate.

"Woo-hoo!" Amber shouts as she runs up, followed by your other teammates.

"You did it!" Riley says, giving you a high five.

"But we knocked down a rail," you confess. "We won't get a ribbon."

"So what?" Shelby says. "The two of you looked amazing."

You grin. It *was* amazing. You asked for help when you needed it. Your friends were there for you when you needed them. And you tackled those showing fears. The confidence you feel right now is your prize, and you know it's worth more than any ribbon.

The End

You invite the team to your room that night. You eat popcorn and play your favorite tunes. When Amber tells everyone that you're riding Sky in the show, the girls cheer. Then Devin starts talking about winning, and Shelby pipes up about beating Hillside. Your head starts to spin.

Amber jumps up. "Hey, guys. Saturday shouldn't be all about winning," she says. "We need to have fun, too."

You stand next to her. "I'm with Amber," you say.

Devin shrugs and looks away.

Later, though, you and Devin dance together to the Strawberries. "I love this song!" she exclaims.

"Me too," you say with a big smile. You and Devin start showing each other your silliest dance moves. Pretty soon, you're both laughing so hard that you have to sit down.

"I like this team-bonding stuff," Devin admits.

You agree. After tonight, you're feeling much better about Devin, and about Saturday's show.

 Turn to page 79.

Sky canters smoothly toward the warm-up fence. Suddenly, your button pops off. Your hunt coat falls open, flapping like wings. Startled, you jerk back on the reins. Sky takes off awkwardly, hits the top rail, and lands hard. When he trots off on the other side, his gait is no longer smooth.

"Something's wrong," Amber hollers. "Pull him up!"

You halt and dismount, and Amber hurries into the ring. Bending over, she lifts up Sky's leg and inspects his hoof. "His shoe's bent. That means we'll have to scratch him from the class," Amber says, her voice thick with frustration.

You don't have to jump Sky in the show after all! You fight the urge to smile.

"That means no points in the Junior Jumper class," Amber says, frowning. "Without those points, the team can't win. Everyone's going to be so disappointed."

Suddenly, you feel awful. This was all your fault! You avoided practicing on Sky because you were too scared. You overslept, and then you even forgot your hunt coat.

"I'll wait here with Sky while the farrier fixes his shoe," Amber says. "Can you tell the others what happened?"

You walk slowly toward the ring, dreading talking with your teammates. But as you think about the past week, you quicken your pace. If there's one thing you've learned, it's that avoiding your fear doesn't make things better—it just makes things worse. *Time to face your fears,* you tell yourself. And facing your teammates is a good first step.

The End

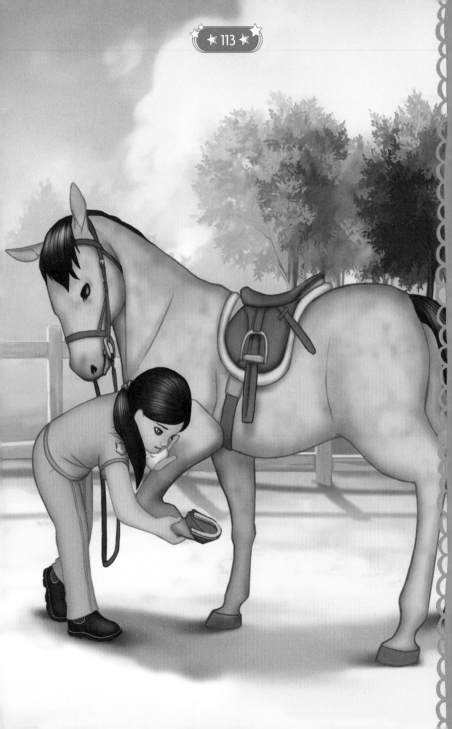

That night, you and Amber pore over the horse show program. "How about a Trail class?" says Amber, pointing halfway down the list. She reads the description. "Horse and rider have to walk over a bridge and through a pretend stream. And open a gate and a mailbox. The horse also has to handle going over poles and around barrels."

"Sounds like fun!" you say, and you mean it.

The next day, you lead Sky to the arena. Riley, Amber, and Shelby wave at you. "Look at this!" Amber calls.

Sky startles at the strange sights. There's a blue blanket on the ground for a stream. A sheet of wood makes a bridge. And in the corner, there's even a mailbox. You laugh. Your friends have set up a crazy obstacle course!

All week, you and Sky practice the course. He learns to stand quietly while you pull a letter from the mailbox and open and shut the gate. He seems to really trust you.

The day of the competition, your stomach does flip-flops, but your confidence blooms when you see the course. There's a blue blanket on the ground, a bridge, and a mailbox to open, just as you and Sky practiced! Then you see it—a big log to jump. *Uh-oh.* Your heart thumps like hoof-beats on that wooden bridge. Part of you wants to gallop out of the ring, but another part knows you can do this.

"Okay, Sky, let's show them what we can do," you whisper. He flicks his ears, listening, and strides forward. Eagerly, he walks across the bridge and the blanket. You pluck the letter from the mailbox and hand it to the judge. Then you open and shut the gate without a hitch. Grinning, you pat Sky, but your smile fades when you turn toward the log. It looms before you as if it were ten feet tall.

Clucking, you trot Sky toward the log. You stare straight ahead, picturing yourself riding through the woods. Sky takes off and jumps the log perfectly.

When you trot Sky from the ring, you're grinning from ear to ear. You thank Amber for helping you find the right class for you. "The Trail class was perfect," you say.

The judge agrees. When the announcer calls the winners, Silver Sky's name is first. You've won a blue—and ten points for the team!

The End

You wait for Riley, Shelby, and Amber in the stable.

"Why so glum?" Shelby asks.

"I really messed up. Sorry, guys," you tell them.

"It's okay," Amber says. "Next show, I'll make sure you walk the course first."

"Next show?" you ask.

Amber holds up her cast. "There's a small show next weekend," she says, "and I won't be ready to compete."

Your mouth falls open. "You want me to ride Sky again?" you ask. "After what happened?"

"Definitely," says Amber, smiling. "Before you went off course, you two rocked."

A second chance, you tell yourself. You've learned what *not* to do this week. Next time, you'll get it right. Your stomach flutters when you think about another show, and this time, it's a flutter of excitement—not fear.

The End

The team gathers around Riley and Sky. Everyone's chattering about the show. "Sky should win a ribbon with you on him," you hear Devin say to Riley.

You feel a twinge of jealousy. That could have been you on Sky.

Then Amber comes to stand next to you. She sighs. "I wish I were the one riding Sky on Saturday," she says.

Amber looks really upset. You've been so focused on yourself that you forgot that your friend can't ride, either.

"You'll be able to ride again soon, right?" you ask.

"Not for a few months," Amber says with a sigh. "But by then, maybe you'll be ready to ride, too."

Instantly, your fears return. "I don't know," you say.

"On Angel," Amber suggests. "The two of you are really good together."

Amber's right. You and Angel *do* make a good team. Tomorrow you'll tell the riding instructor you'd like more jumping lessons. Then maybe, someday soon, you'll be ready to tackle those horse show fears head-on.

The End

You spend the next hour washing, drying, and walking Sky. Then you let him graze by the side of the barn. By then, the show is winding down. Riley has won a second place on Rio. Devin has won a first-place blue and third-place yellow. Shelby has third- and fourth-place ribbons. You, however, got eliminated.

Sighing, you lay your arm over Sky's neck. He's happily munching grass. Worse than getting eliminated was forgetting to take care of your horse.

"Sky looks beautiful," Amber says as she walks out of the stable. "Thank you for bathing him."

"Thank you for not chewing me out," you say. "I deserved it."

Amber shrugs. "Things could have gone better," she admits.

You sigh again. "If I could, I'd start the whole day over," you say.

"The whole day wasn't a disaster," Amber says. "Before you went off course, you and Sky looked terrific together."

"We did?" you say softly. Your sagging confidence lifts a little.

"You did," says Amber. "You'll definitely be ready to ride in the next show."

The thought makes you smile. "Today was crazy," you say, "but it taught me what *not* to do. Next show, I'll be ready to do it right."

The End